The Seven Ci₁

Rheingold

Carl David Mclean

TO RHIAN LLOYD EVANS-MCLEAN

ON OUR WEDDING DAY

WITH LOVE

Also, to our three girls - the sisters of our story.

Evie Dawn Mclean

Rosie May Mclean

and

Jemeima Evans

Part 1

PROLOGUE

The most potent necromancer ever to have walked the face of this earth was a man if you could call him a man, called Rheingold. He had no middle or last name. He did not need any. His name, when uttered correctly, was enough to send a shiver down the spine of anyone familiar with the stories. I'm talking, obviously, about the legend of the Seven Circles.

Many who had heard the stories of The Seven Circles had easily dismissed them as a myth. The power of the Seven Circles was something that our ancestors invented. They invented those centuries ago to scare young children at the hands of their mothers and fathers. They would warn their children that Rheingold that most callous and evil warlock could wield through the Seven Circles, a monstrous power that could defy the natural order of things on this earth.

Some believed in the power of the Seven Circles. These people had interpreted the stories as being nightmares of young children. Those nightmares had, in turn, created the horrific potential of the Seven Circles. This theory may have been correct. These unsuspecting terrors of young children had fueled this magic. They did so as they closed their eyes on an incredibly stormy night while lying in the sanctuary of their beds. While asleep, they can hear the wind blowing against windowpanes throwing and thrashing branches like twiggy witches' fingers scraping on the glass, threatening them. Those children, during their sleep, in turn, would dream of horrific nightmares which would assuredly influence the potency of the Seven Circles.

Some people could not care less about the stupid story of the Seven Circles. It was these moronic people who went about with their lives without a care in the world. They could not comprehend the possibility of such things.

It did not matter what your opinion of it was. I knew the truth.

When I was a young girl, I never believed them, but now, knowing what I know and seeing what I have seen. I believe. I well and genuinely believe.

There is a lot of controversy over where The Seven Circles came from. The main story of their providence started with Rheingold. He was such a powerful sorcerer. He had mastered the arts of many different angles of magic, but he was not satisfied. He wanted his power to match those of the Gods.

Legend had foretold that Rheingold had deceived the Seven Gods of Olympus into creating the Circles. The Seven Circles were given to humankind by the Gods allowing them sanctuary and hope against the forces of darkness which consistently threatened them. The Circles were indeed mighty, and each one possessed the power of the Gods. If the wrong pair of hands were to claim the Circles, those hands would have the ability to defeat the Gods and take control of the heavens, the earth, and the planets.

When they were given to Rheingold, disguised as a lord of the Heavens, he morphed into his proper form as a hooded figure, faceless and evil. He disappeared in a flash. Knowing he had tricked them, the

Gods descended on Rheingold in the Underworld, and a massive battle ensued. At one end stood seven Gods wearing their armored finery, and at the other stood the faceless fiend protected by all manner of beasts of the night. There in front of him stood the snarling evil of those beasts. He had created them with the circles which he had stolen. They all fought amidst the acidic ash of that place.

During the onslaught, Rheingold retreated, knowing that he was no match for the Seven Gods combined. When Zeus, the King of the Gods and ruler of Olympus, realised that Rheingold had easily deceived him. He vowed that no man or beast would ever possess the power of the rings. Therefore, Zeus banished them deep into the ancient lands. He placed three circles in Annwfn, the Celtic Underworld, three in the mortal world and one he kept by his side for the rest of eternity, as he was sure that no one being would ever deceive him again. Without the power of the seven circles combined, there would be no one in this world, Annwfn or the Supreme world, who could ever defeat him.

And Rheingold? Rheingold was banished to Annwfn, the Underworld, lingering in limbo, between the worlds of the dead and the living for eternity.

Or so everyone thought.

And that is where I come in.

CHAPTER 1

THE QUARRY

A slight wind blew the fallen leaves from the trees of Glasfryn Mews. This village was idyllic, and many people said that the Gods created it from the clay of Cae Myrddin and gifted it for the God-fearing people to reside.

The village stood proudly, neighbored by vast forests, calm reservoirs, and picturesque canals painted with an incomprehensible pallet of colours.

Glasfryn Mews, however, had a scourge on the land. This eyesore was Glasfryn Quarry which was partially closed ten years ago. It just did not belong there. The green metallic monstrosity stood prouder, showing off its horrible arrangement of lifts, corrugated sheets and ramps which went deep into the ground.

Something was not right about this day, metamorphosizing in the wind, and changing the air to a thin swirl, making it harder to breathe in. Henry Persey took a short breath before starting the long walk into shaft one at Glasfryn Quarry. He was on his own, and that is how he liked it. As he slowly made his way into the cylindrical tunnel, he never would have believed that today was his last.

It was worth remembering that Henry Persey was a bit of a liar. He was not a bad man, but he would often bend or embellish the truth. Unfortunately, he did that quite often. Over the years, this behaviour led to friends leaving him, with many co-workers not wishing to give an audience to his cons anymore.

Persey had finally arrived at the spot that he had been picking at for the past few days. But, first, he had to get this wall down. Then, he had to pick at it much harder. Very quickly, he had become filthy and hot while mining this part. But he knew that this part of the Quarry was old, and in the ancient rock, deep down, there were big rewards to acquire.

Not long after Henry Percy started the back-breaking task of picking out the rock, he struck something which chinked his pickaxe. Upon inspection with his fingers, a sizeable weak spot had appeared on the face of the stone. He hurriedly thumped his pickaxe into the shallow rock. The thin gravel-like rock crumbled to the ground and as he pulled back his metal pick. He was bewildered as to what it could be. He threw his pick onto the floor with the excitement and trepidation of a teenager. He pulled more of the rock onto the floor with his large hands, black with the coal soot. He gouged repeatedly, excitedly. There had been gold infrequently discovered over the years. These discoveries were old gold, and that was the most valuable. As Glasfryn was the oldest Quarry for miles around, the possibilities of old gold being here were more probable. He smiled to himself and thought how well off he would be if he found just one small cluster of gold. He would never tell anyone of his discovery. There were no check-ins or strip searches at the Quarry, so he could quickly get away with the theft. This plan had been in his head for a while.

He repeated his scooping process quickly until the black background of the hole turned grey. He scooped more until the grey turned to a much paler shade. It was a few minutes before the speckled grey had turned to an exceptionally light grey, and then came the smell. It was the smell of sulphur and burning that he had never sensed in his life before. Then, a weak beam of red light started to shine through on his face as he pulled the last fragments of the rock back.

The light turned to soft red and then a brighter red until the light hurt his eyes in contrast to the Quarry's dimly lit tunnels.

He was momentarily blinded, and he drew back to his knees. He had started to find it hard to breathe, and he held his hand in his lap as a horrible feeling came over him. He felt the presence of something behind him, and he froze. He nervously turned his shoulders to see what it was, and he was relieved to see that there was nothing there.

He started to compose his fat body up to the hole in the rock to see what was there. He was so excited, and he was going to be so rich. He peered through the hole into the chasm of the red glow. He squinted his eyes and partially covered his face with his left hand. He could smell that sulphur much stronger now, and the feeling of impending doom had started to become increasingly apparent around him.

He sensed a presence behind him again, but now on his right-hand side. Similarly, but more nervously, he quickly turned to see who was there. But, once more, there was nothing. He wiped his brow, which was now perspiring as the rock's warm heat slowly and surely got hotter and hotter.

He peered around again to the hole he had proudly made. This time, the smoke was starting to clear, and he could make out the faint shadow of a man dressed in a shroud floating a good ten metres in the air amidst the red glow. As the figure became more apparent, Percy could see that the cloaked figure was waving his arms in mid-air, thrashing, and swirling through the billowing smoke. He was conducting the most demonic symphony any human had ever heard. Moreover, there was nothing human about this figure. Henry Percy quickly pulled his body back with his grim realisation that he was staring into the fires of Hell.

As Percy looked on in horror, the shroud's deep and booming voice filled the void of that massive congregation. As the smoke cleared a little, he could make out a vast cauldron with green mist floating over the top and spewing down the sides. Persey could not make out the words, but he did not need to. Nobody would have required any comprehension of the words to know that it was a ritual from Hell itself. He knew this was sorcery of the worst kind.

The hooded being arched, his back suspended in mid-air. He paused and propelled his chest forward, throwing his arms forward in the direction of the cauldron. A burst of flames shot out from the shroud's fingertips like red lightning. The blaze joined and hung over the vat for a moment. Henry Percy could make out the demented shapes of horribly disfigured people. The damned. They were floating from the fiery chasms and joining the flame pool. Then came the words.

"resurgemus antiquis bestia me et Romam reuerterunt"

Suddenly, a shriek came out of the fiery wisps, a groaning that Percy had never heard or ever will again. The cries were unbearable, and that poor man struggled to cover his ears. The demonic and foul voice shrieked again.

"Veni mi bestia. Audi me, et resurget ex favilla et inferos"

The sound now pounded every part of that craggy place. The horrific cries from the damned swirled around the cavern and then mutated into a colossal howl. From the cauldron, two massive claws shot out of the steam and grabbed each of the sides. Then. Nothing. Darkness returned, accompanied by the silence. It was the most profound silence.

Henry Persey found himself on his back after being so terrified, stumbling, in disbelief of what he had seen. The orchestra of Hell had come to an abrupt tacet.

Persey did not know what to think and what to do? His brain tried processing a million emotions, which was swirling behind his eyes. It made no sense. It was not real. What should he do? Should he call the police? Run like the movies, running out of the tunnel, screaming? Would any sane person believe him?

Before he could decide, he sniffed in a foul smell through his nose, which instantly filled him with dread. He froze. The sensation of something considerable approaching grew and grew. Henry's mind had paralysed him on the spot. He could only move his head haltingly and carefully while suddenly becoming aware of a low sounding growl. He tried to run, but the Beast displayed its pair of powerful claws, incorporating powerful tendons which allowed him to clamp around Henry Persey's head. Without any fuss, the Beast's thumbs slit through Henry's face allowing him the grip to quickly divide Henry's skull with the irresistible force of his hellish might. Blood splattered the tunnel walls. Fragmented pieces of bone dripped in between the capillaries of the red matter, slowly running, and drying on the rock.

This massacre was the start of the Beast's rampage.

CHAPTER 2

ELLIE-MAY PROTHEROE

It was a cold Friday night when it first happened. It was a horrible night that everyone in the village would never forget. Ellie-May Protheroe had started walking from her friend's 16th birthday party an hour before it was over. She left before everyone else at the party had even realised that she had gone. She left before the others, but she would be the last one to arrive home.

The chilly wind bit at her face as she walked through the darkness. Her house was close to the party, but she was starting to realise that the journey was taking far too long. Her legs were heavy, and she needed as much energy as she could to move them. She felt uneasy that she had not consumed that much alcohol, which started to worry her. As in, she was alone. Alone. She had briefly stumbled to the floor, holding out her hands outstretched to slow her fall in case her head would hit the damp concrete. She felt the cold wet of the rain among the prickled craters of the uneven mortar. She brushed herself off sheepishly as she got to her feet, briskly turning around to check that nobody had witnessed her foolishness.

She had left the party before everyone else because of Danny. That horrible sick son of a bitch, who had been talking to his friends about her. She knew what they were discussing while his hand shielded his mouth. She could not lipread, but she just knew. She also noticed that her friendship group were being distant from her. It started when they said they would meet her there, but they all turned up together after her. She could tell by their subtle over-confident manner that they had done their usual thing of sucking down a few bottles of alcohol down by the park. That is what she always did with them. But now, she was not with them, and she did not know why they would treat her like that. She could feel the consistent stabbing of their eyes on her back as they flirted with the boys. They were all standing together, laughing, touching, and talking about her, Ellie-May Protheroe and Danny Jones, the boy who had done nothing wrong. It was all her fault. It was she who deserved everything that she got.

She and Danny were complicated. It was a complicated situation that she found herself in. Ellie-May thought that she had more friends than she currently did, and she never thought that they would turn against her and betray her in this way.

She was going up to the tunnel as the rain was still spitting down harder and harder, stinging her arms. She should have worn a coat, she thought to herself. She should have listened to her dad. She was now in a familiar part of the village. This place was where she and Danny would usually be many times after school previously, but not now.

Ellie-May looked up ahead towards the tunnel entrance and across from the light, which shone the last beam of hope of enlightenment before she dipped into darkness. Those kids who had smashed those lights a few months before had not realised the terror they would have caused her. But there she was, alone, unsteady and bewildered by the trees.

Those streets looked so beautiful as like dancers with outstretched fingers swaying violently and whistling veraciously amidst the black hopelessness of that Friday night. Ellie-May took one step forwards and two steps back, and the idea came to her mind that some sicko may have drugged her at the party.

No way! That type of thing does not happen in our lovely little village. She had taken her drinks, opened her bottles and drank her alcohol. She was not that neglectful to allow that to have happened. Especially her.

But why did she feel so hopeless? It was because those bitches had forced her to leave the party early. She had hoped that she could have sorted things out with Danny. He was her love and her first love at that. She cherished him.

Why was he whispering to Katrina, whispering past her ear as she caressed her curly hair?

Why did her head pound so much? She had convinced herself that she had not fallen victim to drugging.

Why had she suddenly felt so scared?

It was because, unknowingly to her, she was walking into a trap!

She was walking into the darkness, which would change her life forever, and she started to tremble at the feeling of being so cold, wet, and alone in the dark. She remembered the dancing trees again, tempting her to dance. But she did not feel like dancing. That is what she told the boys at the party, and that is how she still felt now. She remembered her dad also, standing in the front doorway, telling her to be home on time, why she did not take her health seriously, and why she did not take a bloody jacket on God's earth. She was soaking now, and her hair was a matted mess on the sides of her face. Her mascara had started to run; her lipstick had faded. She looked like a mess where once she had thought that she looked stunning. She looked like her mother. She still remembered how her mother looked, smelt, and sounded. She was just like her, slim, blonde, and beautiful.

She was in the darkness, and she was soaking wet. The material of her cyan blouse had turned dark blue and heavy, but she could not see it.

Suddenly, and without warning, something did not feel right. Ellie-May thought that she could hear what she thought sounded like a car engine. Its low, dull monotone humming sound before you press the accelerator. But she realised very quickly that there were no cars around.

She stopped, dead in her tracks and attempted to identify the sound that she was hearing. That humming was so clear, but she could not put her finger on what it was. Then a louder pant-like breath, like the sound a train makes when coming into the station. Her eyes drew closer to a dark shadow that had manifested unclearly near a large bush that grew unevenly at the tunnel's side. She was drawn to it and bewildered at the same time as to what exactly it could be. Next, there sounded a significant rustle of the leaves, which was getting louder and louder. There was also that car noise, which sounded more like a cat - a loud cat purring before pouncing.

Then the shape of the sound changed, and it sounded more like a dog. A mad dog, unhappy, now starting to snarl. She suddenly noticed a cloud of what she understood was a foggy breath when warm air hits the cold that spread over the top of the horrible bush. Someone was there, crouching and had started to pull back the twiggy leaves.

Then, in the blink of her blue eyes, the rainfall that took solace on the green leaves exploded as a giant mass burst out of the bush with a loud howl. For what seemed like hours, the beast stood there about fifty yards from her. The grey mane around its massive neck glistened amid the full moon. It crouched momentarily on its muscular hind legs; its toes spread on the surface of the tarmac as if to anchor its vast shape on the ground. It arched its hairy back and outstretched its arms displaying all its horrific wonder. The beast's claws were long and twiggy but unlike the trees. They were full of massive veins and terrible ligaments and muscle, which forced them to twitch back and forth, revealing the sharpest implements of doom she had ever seen. It was terror personified, and that little girl was helpless, frozen, and dumb. Then, suddenly, its giant footsteps smashed the floor with the weight of what sounded like a hundred men. She was in slow motion, and as she picked up her hands to rub her eyes to see when it would strike, that massive dark shape was running at her. The last thing she remembered was seeing the blur of his claws forcefully rip through her chest. She felt a dull ache and the sound of something wet and heavy fall in front of her feet. The beast stood firm, and its large eyes pierced her being. She could feel the warm trickle of her urine pour down her legs. It sniffed again, hunched again, as it let out a massive, fearless scream to the moon as if to damn the curse which would not allow this girl to live.

She looked down at her feet, and she understood that her tormentor had disemboweled her. With a quick thud from its left arm, punching forcefully at her throat, launching her tiny and frail body into the air until she landed on her back, her head smashed against the tarmac. The assault was quick, unforgiving, and cruel, but she did not feel any pain. It was only the slow fade of her beating heart, which told her that she was dying. She felt a warm sensation fill her chest in her last moments, and it was sticky to the touch. The blood pooled up through her veins, creating mini reservoirs in the claw marks which reached from under her throat down to her belly. As she lay on the warm concrete floor, she knew enough about the world to see that she would not live another day. The beast stepped up again slowly, inquisitively, towards where she lay. As her eyes closed, before she fell into the void, she remembered for one last time the face of her mother, who she missed and her dad, who loved her - and Danny. Her first and only true love. Danny, that bastard, son of a bitch.

CHAPTER 3

THE PARTY

Ellie-May had left the party at eight o clock, and only one person saw and noticed that she had left. Only one person saw her walk out of the back door, through the small garden and the side gate. The name of that person was Katrina Proust. There was one thing that everyone in this village had come to understand about Katrina Proust and her vicious upper-middle-class family. They were the lowest of the low. They were immoral, but they were rich. And in this world, especially in this village, their wealth had bought them certain concessions. Their family unit was the biggest and most terrible cliche of the modern world. The father, Nigel Proust, was a wealthy businessperson. He owned businesses. Nobody in the village ever suspected how he acquired those businesses and the lengths he had gone in the past to purchase them. Take his most recent conquest, a small family-run tech shop in the heart of the local community. He wanted to own and possess the business. He had asked them by way of a legal letter of his intention to buy the company. But they declined. The family thought very highly of the offer, but it was a rouse, a lie. He did not want the business at that price. He wanted it much lower. So, he contracted a gang from the nearest town. He paid them handsomely for them to put the frighteners on that local shop. It first started with some petty theft from the store. They then mugged the old guy who owned the place when he was locking up one night. I mean, mugging a man outside a place where he has been most comfortable all his life. It is immoral. But Nigel Proust was never suspected. The family, however, were proud people and determined not to give up. So those gang of petty criminals took things up a notch. One night, they broke into the store, smashed it up and set it alight.

The owners rushed to the scene when they received the call from the police telling them of the fire. You could imagine their hearts crushing, thinking of all their blood, sweat and tears melting away in the immense heat of the flames. The old guy, in the end, decided to sell to Proust, and he accepted forty per cent less. As he put it, Proust was buying a ton of ash and scorch marks where the shop used to be, which was correct. But, somehow, Proust intimidated the insurance company into paying up, and he built a brand-new store that is the biggest and best for miles around. That is just one story of Nigel Proust. His word means shit.

His daughter, Katrina, was not even in her father's league. But she was in training. The way she spoke to people, even her so-called friends, was horrible. Plus, she was fake. She had fake friends, fake family, and a much more phony life. She was envious of everyone, and she had to have what was coveted by others, just like her father. If it was not 'Instagramable', 'Facebookable' or 'Snapchatable', it was not right, and it certainly was not worthy of her time and attention. And more than anything, she loved to put her filthy nose into other people's business, just like her father.

She saw Ellie-May escape through the back door at the party. She had left because of her. Ellie-May had left because Katrina Proust was dripping off her ex-boyfriend like fake jewels worn by a witch. Katrina did not understand the fundamental bond of love and friendship that Ellie-May and

Danny had established over the years. She knew that she wanted to destroy it. She had taken a shine to Danny incredibly early in the school year. Katrina had made her feelings noticeably clear to him even in front of Ellie-May, which had ended up in a fight outside the school gates about a fortnight ago. But Mr. Proust had made it clear to the school who was to blame. This war did not go down too well with him, having his daughter sat outside the Headteacher's office facing charges of assault. But when all is said and done, it is money that is more powerful than the truth, and Ellie May took a two-week exclusion. Katrina got away with it and remained in school to twist and manipulate the story ensuring Ellie-May was an outcast from social circles. Danny's dad insisted on the couple's separation. They would never be allowed to be seen in public again, or else he would lose his job. He was the store manager at the tech store. Just recently been promoted. Nobody loved this series of events more than Katrina Proust. That horrible brat of a girl.

Katrina knew that she had done her job as she saw that blonde skinny bitch walk out of that party early. She knew that she had successfully driven her out of Danny's life and that he and so unbeknown to him opened another door with her. He was standing in the doorway, but he would be walking step by step closer towards her in time. All she knew was that Danny was hers for the taking, and she intended to take him that night at the party during that full moon that hung so pendulously heavy and beautifully in the sky.

She turned back to the party, picked up a bottle of alcohol and said aloud but hidden by the sound of the music.

"I'm going to claim my prize. He's mine".

As she paced down the hallway to where the party was at its hottest, she paused as if to wonder where her other two friends had gone. She pulled her mobile out of her side pocket and frantically texted her entourage. Seconds later, they appeared, scuttling like tiny crabs towards her.

"This party is so bad". Look at all these insignificant idiots", exclaimed Katrina.

Her malice dripped slowly off her tongue, like black tar. The twins looked at each other but did not dare say a word. Their only solemn responsibility was to agree with Katrina and to nod and hang off her every word. And the worst thing about this friendship was that they understood the putrid imbalance of social power that Proust wielded over them.

"Where has Danny got to?" questioned Katrina, expecting an expeditious answer. None came.

She quickly understood that she was not going to get the required information from Dilly and Dally. So, Katrina turned on her heels and stormed off in search of her plaything, Danny.

Danny was upstairs, talking to his mates. He looked at a sleek and horrible movement on the stairs and quickly noticed that it was Katrina who was making a beeline straight for him with lust and languish in her eyes.

He knew what she was after, but he was not going to give into her. Not this time. He briefly thought of his dad, and hen Ellie-May, the love of his life. No, not anymore. It was just so unjust. It was not charming the way that Proust had a hold over his old man. But then, Danny thought from a third-person perspective that his dad must have felt demoralised to have his childhood bully still be in charge. Danny and his dad had quarreled many nights over the unjustness, but he understood that he had to give in as his dad was a single parent and finances have been ever so tight recently.

As she reached the top of the stairs and briefly paused for a breath, Katrina pointed her index finger at him and pulled it towards her, hooking Danny like a little fish out of its depth. He did not wish to talk to her again as he had been hiding from her. He had been quite successful until now, but she had found him. Danny did not wish to see her again tonight. Katrina had already made a move on him while she whispered into his ear downstairs. Danny could still smell cigarette tobacco on the lapel of his shirt. She had left her mark on him. He did not want to be polite or even be in the same space as her. Danny knew that he had to keep the peace and keep the Proust's happy. He had memorised that from his dad.

As he dutifully approached her, her tone softened.

"I hope you're not ignoring me"? she said suggestively.

"Why can't we go somewhere to talk in private?" She purred through her teeth and past her lips.

"I've been waiting to get you alone for ages", she said.

Danny's heart sunk into his chest as he comprehended what Katrina was after. There was part of him who loved hearing the compliment, but it came from the wrong girl. He knew that there would be many boys at this party who would have loved Katrina to be talking to them. But she was talking to Danny, and he hated it. He did not want to give in to her. He did not want anything to do with her or her cruel father. They were like cancer to him. But he shut his mouth, and as she lifted her hand and grabbed his hand in hers, placing it on her bare chest where her blouse separated in the middle. He concluded that he had to go with the flow to keep his dad happy. They had to keep the money coming in. They had to survive. He closed his eyes for what seemed like a lifetime, slowly easing his body into hers as he kissed her unwillingly on her seductive red lips.

Within a flash, Katrina pulled onto the lapel of Danny's shirt and tugged him into a doorway.

CHAPTER 4

UNWANTED GUESTS

The party was in full swing at half-past eight when the three sisters paced purposefully through the front door, they had flung open. They strode unapologetically through the hallway across the most beautifully polished parquet flooring, which was laid by Proust's wealth. Many so-called friends were uninvited to the party, but they had used the side door. Ellie-May had used the same door a good half an hour before the arrival of the three sisters.

The three sisters had turned up to the party, knowing that they were uninvited, but they were there to see two people. The first and most important person was their newly acquired friend, Ellie-May.

The sisters had never spoken with Ellie-May during school. They had discovered her sobbing her heart out in the toilets after Danny ended their relationship. Her love life had ended, and her life was crumbling around her among the foul smell of stale urine. They had invested time in Ellie-May and had supported her when there was nobody in whom to turn. It was a most unlikely of friendships, but they had been there for her. They were her solace.

That very evening, Ellie-May had texted the eldest of the sisters, Delilah. Since as far back as she could remember, she had hated her name and had recently insisted on being referred to as Leila. When Leila received the text, she summoned the other two to attend and to order. They paced through the night to the home of Katrina Proust, their number one arch enemy. They had hated her forever. She was everything they were not, wealthy, and filthy rich. However, they were everything she was not, kind, considerate and loving. There was also one thing. These sisters were not afraid of anyone.

Leila received Ellie-May's text an hour previously. The message read that Katrina Proust had been trying to get her way with Danny all night, provoking Ellie-May with suggestive and dirty looks. Ellie-May could not stand it. Leila had also interpreted the text as a cry for help. She had to get there quickly before something terrible happened.

The second person who would face the wrath of the sisters was Danny. They wanted to have a word with him. They could not believe that Danny would have ever treated Ellie-May like this. First finishing their relationship and, secondly, falling for the allures of Katrina, who was taking him like a lamb to the slaughter. If Katrina Proust could get her hands on him, there would be no return for Ellie-May.

In their view, he was a two-faced liar. Nobody knew what was going on, but all the three sisters knew was that their friend Ellie May had to be at the party, and they wanted to put an arm around her to tell her that everything was going to be all right and that they were there to support her in any way she wanted it.

This side was the more amenable and caring side of the sisters. On the one hand, they were caring and loving girls, and on the other side, they were badass bitches. They did not say things wonderful things when there were nasty people around. They were excellent judges of character. They got that from their father. But when there were despicable people involved, they would fight. That was something to behold. Although they had the name of 3 sisters, they were not sisters. Delilah was the eldest of the three sisters, Emsie was the youngest of the two sisters. To complete the trio was Crystal, their stepsister. Crystal was a product of their father's recent union with the local school counselor, Nancy Partridge.

It was safe to say that the older two sisters were not always changeable in character. They had to adapt to new situations. They were astute in school but did not shine in glory. Their intelligence was entirely a matter of fact to them. The older two sisters had become rebellious against their father, and they did not know why.

They had gotten older. When the clock struck on the girl's sixteenth birthday, their father had become an average person. The magic of childhood had unveiled the reality. For years, their father was a giant, a fearless warrior in the world. Now, with age, they had discovered that he was ordinary. He had a familiar face, a regular job, and an everyday life. He also had normal daughters.

Their father appeared to them now as a mortal. He had no armor, and he was able to die. For years, they had always thought that he would be everlasting. Nature had declared that the world had made him, and he would pass on this earth when it was his time. The grim reality of life had shattered childhood's dream.

The sisters, now facing the party's congregation, all looking at them, uneasy and wondering what they were doing there and what they wanted. The dumb silence broke with Leila.

"Proust", she screamed at the top of her voice with a mixture of womanhood and razor blades that protruded through her mouth, with spit shooting out intermittently through small spaces in her lips.

Her step-sister Crystal followed.

"Proust, you bitch!

Her sister, Emsie, looked at her, shocked that her half-sister had used such a disgusting word.

"Do you have to use language like that, Crys?" Crystal looked at her, puzzled by Emsie's question.

"Duh. Yes," replied Crystal, giving Emsie a slight pull on her arm as to warn her not to embarrass her in front of the crowd. Leila quickly interjected.

"Will you two get your shit together?" Her tongue hissed through her teeth.

"We are here for Ellie-May. Get a grip".

The younger sisters looked back at each other and nodded in agreement. They did not want to be at this house. They did not belong there. They had to get Ellie-May out of there as quickly as possible.

After a brief pause, a boy from the crowd, propped up by a mahogany cabinet, raised his arm, then his hand, then outstretched his short and stubby index finger towards the top of the stairs.

"I saw her earlier upstairs with Danny".

The youngest two looked at Leila, and the three stepped swiftly towards the stairs and firmly paced up the steps two at a time. When they ascended at the top step, Emsie looked left and then right. Paused and raised a slow breath through her lips. She put her hands on her hips to assist her in her thinking.

"This place is huge! How many rooms have they got?".

Crystal squared up to a large girl who had been minding her own business, enjoying the party. There were spilt alcohol stains from the top of her white polo neck top, and she looked dazed.

"Where is Katrina bloody Proust?" She whispered into the chin of the girl who stood taller than her. Although the height may have been different, there was no mistake that the three sisters could handle themselves. Rumours of the sister's aggressive nature had been consistent in the school over the past five years. Were any of them true? Only the three of them knew. That said, the three sisters basked in the fear.

"She's in there", she pointed to the door, which had welcomed Katrina and Danny a while before the girls' unwanted attendance.

The three strutted towards the door, and Leila tried pushing the handle downwards quickly while at the same time pushing her right shoulder into it. Her leather coat cushioned part of the pain. She knew that she had to make an entrance. A grand show.

Thankfully, Katrina had not locked the room. Leila flicked her wrist, forcing the heavy wood forwards until it thudded on the wall at the other side. The three sisters stepped into the room, dimly lit apart from two bedside lamps' warm glow. The light covered a massively luxurious bed, seductively draped by the most delicate silk sheets. In the bed, two bodies that stretched arms had previously entwined shot up with a refractory shock.

"What the hell!" screamed Katrina.

"What the hell do you three inbreeds think you're doing?"

Katrina was frantically pulling the thin bra straps back over her shoulders and fumbling out of bed, correcting her jean buttons.

"Where's Ellie-May?", asked Leila directing her question to the two lovers.

She looked at Danny, who had started to pull his body over to the side of the bed. He was putting his shirt on, which she had flung on the floor. Leila looked straight at him.

"I can't believe you've done this" her eyes started to well up as she thought of the evident betrayal.

"I'm not doing anything wrong", retorted Danny. "Ellie-May and I have finished".

There was something not right about Danny. He was slurring his words as if he were drunk, but his eyes held a glowing green secret. His head did not seem right on his shoulders. It was like he had been drugged.

"What is wrong with him?" Whispered Emsie to her sisters.

"I don't know", answered Leila.

The three sisters knew that something was not right, and the air was thin. They just could not put their finger on it. They were there for Ellie-May, and she had disappeared. Danny seemed to be drugged, and it just did not add up. It started to feel weird.

Katrina slid up to him and comforted him with her warm hand on his shoulder.

"There, there, my love. Don't you worry about a thing. I will see that these bitches leave".

She stood to her feet slowly and made her way towards Emsie. She knew that she was the weaker of the three, and she would be easier to intimidate. So, her tone changed from a scream to a type of playful one.

"Now, now, now. What are we going to do with you three?"

"You can say what you want, but Danny is coming with us." Crystal stepped in front of Katrina as if to act as a barricade in front of Emsie.

"Danny isn't going anywhere", Katrina said playfully.

"He doesn't care about that skank, Ellie-May, and he is staying put," she defiantly finished her sentence by putting her middle finger up at the girls.

The crowd of onlookers started to creep by the door for a glimpse of the commotion. They could not believe what was going on. I mean, people were standing up to Katrina, which made quite a change.

"You put that finger near my face, and you will wish that you hadn't". Leila had started to face the fact that Danny would not come with them and that they were in a house full of Katrina Proust lovers who could mess up the three of them.

This fact suddenly infuriated her, and she started to feel the embarrassment and shame heat up in her chest and started to flow towards her throat. Katrina pushed again.

"You are so full of shit. You have broken into my house, burst into my room, and threatened me in front of my boyfriend"

"I'm not your boyfriend", retorted Danny. I will never be your boyfriend".

He shook his head as he retorted as if to awaken from a bad dream. He looked down at his body and questioned himself. He did not know where he was. He looked up at the girls as if to wonder where he was and how the three sisters were there and how the hell was he in Katrina Proust bedroom with his shirt undone?

"How the Hell could you have done this to Ellie-May?", Emsie shouted at Danny.

He stared at the floor while still trying to piece the last half hour together, but he drew a blank.

"How dare you come into my house!"

"Why are you half-naked ......?"

"Where is Ellie-May?"

"How is she getting home?"

Danny screamed as he clasped his hands over his ears to drown out the noise. All the questions had merged into one dull roar, and it was unbearable. He felt sick and drunk, but he knew that he was not. He looked at Leila, and she stared into his eyes from across the room. Her lips did not move, but he could hear her voice in his head.

"Danny, what has happened?" Whispered Leila.

"Why are you here with her? She asked again.

"I don't know", he replied, secretly.

Leila looked at Danny. How did she hear him speak to her? He had not moved his lips, but she heard him as clear as day. She looked at the others, still arguing with each other. Some of the other partygoers had started to join the argument as it intensified. Leila and Danny stood firm, still in a trans like communicative form.

Suddenly Leila noticed that a glowing sphere of light had started to rise out of her sister, Emsie, as the argument continued. Her face glowed white, and her eyes turned black as if she had begun to take on a demonic form. Leila and Crystal drew back in fear at the sight of her sister's transformation. Leila also noticed that a ball of fire had started to grow from the palms of her hands.

At this point, in the blinking of an eye, the party people noticed what was going on. They started to back off. Crystal stood there, too, realising that some weird things were happening to her sisters. There were exuding energy, but she could only stand there dumb, looking on as it consumed the room.

Seconds later, Katrina Proust took a large breath before she let out a mighty scream. As she cried, the flames from Leila's palms erupted, and Emsie's earthy glow exploded, shattering every window in the room.

The bed was engulfed in flame as it ran uncontrollably up the walls, over the curtains and swirled like a furnace on the ceiling.

Emsie's glow covered the girls and Danny as if to offer loving protection from the flames. Katrina backed towards the window and climbed out onto her balcony, her face black with ash and the red scorches still stinging her face. The girls and Danny stood in the cool glow, but they could still feel the flames' heat but remained unharmed. They looked up at the fire, which was now circling in an anti-clockwise movement on the ceiling. Then, a skull-like hooded figure appeared in flames, and an awful noise arose from the burning chorus of the fire. The hooded figure let out a most wicked and crooked laugh.

"I have found you. Your father did his best to conceal the three of you from me."

Leila looked at the others with a dumb look on her face.

"I WILL BE WAITING FOR YOU", cried the skull. Then, a massive claw-like hand reached for Danny and the three girls.

At this moment, Crystal let out a petrified squeal and jumped onto her sisters and Danny taking hold of their hands as she did so. There was a flash of green mist, and they had disappeared from the room and Proust's house.

CHAPTER 5

I WON'T BELIEVE

"What in God's name had just happened? exclaimed Leila with her hands clapped around her cheeks. She could not believe what had just happened. She could not think that two minutes ago, fire beams had poured out of her fingers. Indeed, that could not have happened.

But it just did.

The three sisters and Danny collected themselves to their feet as the trucks' sirens squealed in the background. Emsie was not concentrating on what had just happened. Instead, she had an uncontrollable urge to get to Ellie-May.

"Her phone is off", sobbed Emsie as she tried again.

Do you realise what has just happened to us?" Leila screamed at Emsie as if losing control of herself momentarily. She stood there, her hands waved through her hair, and she panted for a bit before closing her eyes and counting silently to ten in her head.

"Is anyone listening to me?" said Leila.

"I mean. How the Hell did I burn Katrina Proust's house down?"

She stood there for a moment expecting an answer, but no answer came. They were all dumbfounded.

She started again.

"Can anyone. Just anyone of you explain how the Hell that had just happened?" The emotion was too much for her, and she broke down crying. The others looked at each other, not knowing what to say or do. Leila rattled on nearing hysteria.

"I don't think anyone is listening to me. What has just happened? I've just burned down Proust's house with fire from my fingertips" - she was looking closely at her fingers. There was no sign of fire and no burn marks, residue, or anything to suggest that she had just accomplished such a feat.

Danny perked up.

"Okay, so you've just burned down Proust's house with your fingers, but what I don't understand is how on earth I was in bed with Katrina Proust. The only person in this world I hate"

He stood up straight and wanted an answer, but again, none came.

Crystal piped up with tears in her eyes.

"Guys. I touched your hands, and we all jumped through time and ended up here".

She took solace of a hug in the arms of Emsie, and they both cried together for a while. Crystal muttered again,

"All I did was touch your hands, then we all came here. But I knew where I wanted us to end up. Who can explain this to us?"

Finally, she turned her head to the side and threw up. Everyone looked at her, but nobody commented.

Emsie was still trying her phone in one hand whilst comforting Crystal with the other arm around her. She stopped momentarily,

"Still. That's weird. I don't know what has just happened. Okay, Leila, you have just had fire coming out of your fingers. Emsie, I don't know what happened to you. You had some white glow over you like a ghost. I didn't understand. Then, I transported all of us from the house to this hill. I can't understand it, can you?"

The four kids were stuck, bewildered as they could not comprehend what had just happened, but they had to do one thing. The only thing that mattered to them was to get to Ellie May. They could not have understood it, but something might have happened to her if this night had gone so badly for them.

What was in store for Ellie May?

Where was she?

Who is she with?

Nothing made sense anymore. However, they all had this grand feeling of freedom. They had never felt like this before.

Leila stood up firmly and collected herself. She was the most senior in the group, and she thought it was her responsibility to shed some light on what had happened.

"I know what we should do. Let's get back home before the police pick us up for arson".

CHAPTER 6

HOME SWEET HOME

It was all too much for Danny. That weasel had run off home, saying that he didn't want to play any part of the madness which the girls had created.

It was late when the three sisters arrived home. The three of them meandered up the drive to their house. The backdrop of the night was still transparent, and a misty fog lay lifeless like a blanket on the ground. They strolled towards the large house which stood weakly on the gravel. Crystal opened the door of their home, and they peered around to see who was still up. The light from within the house shone brightly in contrast to the outside, dark and mysterious.

"Dad!" Emsie shouted at the top of her voice. She knew that her dad was up. He was something of a night owl.

"He's probably in the study," Leila said as they started the descent into the lower part of the house.

When they arrived at the bottom of the stairs which had led them into the bowels of their home, Crystal shouted out,

"Dad?" Her voice hung around the basement like a sound in a cave. There was a slight pause and then.

"I'm here. I'm working". replied the frail voice. To anyone else but the three sisters, that sentence may have been quite strange. A person working late into the night. But that is how their dad was. He would often stay up late into the small hours of the morning with his work and then sleep all day when they were at school.

They walked into the office, which sat round to the right-hand side of the basement.

As they entered the room, a small man who looked about fifty but sounded a lot older sat beside a large wooden desk. He was at work, and it was here he was at his happiest. They saw straight away what their dad had been fixing.

On the desk stood a brass cage, and within the enclosure stood the most beautiful brown barn owl the girls had ever seen, which perched lifelessly on the small wooden swing suspended by a small metal chain tied at the top of the cage.

"I'm nearly done". This one has taken me a while. Their dad's voice sounded almost reverent, and there was an air of undeniable mental ability that shrouded his small frame. His voice could have well belonged to an old History professor.

The three sisters hung around the desk, admiring their dad's work. They looked pleased with the bird. But, as they looked around the room, they could also respect the arrangement of stuffed animals and wildlife which had met their untimely demise, which now adorned the darkroom.

"This one is stunning, dad", complemented Crystal, who was still looking at the fine detail of the marble eyes which Dad had put into the sockets about an hour before their return.

"I trust you girls have had an eventful night?" their dad asked. He always wondered in a suspecting manner. It was as if dad knew that the girls had been in trouble. He had suspected something. But they weren't sure. There was no way on God's Earth that he could have predicted, even fathom what had happened to them tonight.

The girls stood silent as if their dad had asked them the most complex and challenging question known to humankind. But they could quickly have answered. Instead, however, they remained still and silent.

"Well?" Their father had been waiting. Not for long, but he wasn't used to waiting at all.

The girls' father was what we would refer to as old-fashioned. He respected the fine things in life, including this excellent barn owl he had been fixing for the best part of six hours. He also appreciated manners. He would always say that well-mannered people would shape the future of this world—the future politicians and scientists. The young people of this world with no manners would not come to anything in life, and that is just how it was.

"Nothing much", Emsie answered after being thudded in the back by Crystal. She did this because she knew that if their father had one weakness, it was Emsie. He loved the girls equally, but there was just something special about Emsie. Of course, that's what the girls thought, and of course, they would never have dared confront him about it.

"Anything else?" Their dad questioned as he was always quite suspicious about his daughters.

There was a silence that hung in the air for a moment before he raised his voice, slamming his hands on the hardwood of the solid table.

"What has been going on?" A thunder-like sound bellowed out of the small man, white droplets of saliva spurted from his lips, and his eyes grew heavy and red.

"It was nothing, dad, we swear," Emsie cried as her father continued to bellow.

Then, there was silence. The three sisters stood like naughty school children as if waiting for the school Principal to hand down some awful sentence.

Their dad slumped into his leather chair and drew a large breath. He waited, and the sisters also waited anxiously. Finally, he spoke.

"My girls. My loves. It is time you knew the truth" He drew another breath as if the weight of a hundred secrets which were waiting to be disclosed from his thin lips. The girls stood, wondering what was going on. This night had been too weird, and they now asked that anything after the human-made fire and teleportation was possible. Their father bowed his head and then looked up and turned his head to face a large portrait on the wall by the side of them. The sisters knew the face of the picture to be the face of their deceased mother. The image still hung as a reminder of past life that was now not spoken about.

He looked at the girls and raised his arms in the air. Then, the light of the electric light weakened until there was total darkness. Then, there was a glimmer of green light that fluttered past the girls' noses. They quickly shot their heads around to see what it was; it had gone. Then, the barn owl on the table blinked and cocked its head under its left-wing and started to pick at the fur with its beak. The girls turned their focus to their dad, who was sitting behind the owl. He was smiling back at them. They knew that they were safe.

"What the …?" Leila's question fell silent as a wood pigeon flew contently past her shoulder. She looked around. All the animals who had sat dead, lay stuffed and miserable were now full of life and energy and enjoying a playtime. All of this was under the direction of their father.

"I know it wasn't going to be long before you were going to find out", their dad said. After that, more animals became curious about the girls, and a red fox stood on Crystal's foot and then lifted his leg and peed on her shoe.

"You little..." she protested, and the fox looked up at her as if giving her a cheeky smile before sauntering off.

They fixed their eyes again on their father. His orbs outstretched as he arose from his seat effortlessly. But then noticed that he was not moving his legs; gravity itself lifted him off the chair. So, they stood again dumb as Dad held his arms aloft and commanded a white force which they had previously seen in Emsie at Proust's house. Then the white spirit turned to fire, and the heat intensified. The animals had noticed the flame-like circle, and some of them cowered not to be harmed. But they knew that their second creator would never let any harm befall them.

"Told us, what? Shouted Crystal. She had to scream as the fire whirred and cracked in front of them. Their father pulled open his arms, making the circle of fire more significant, and in the middle, the ring became solid, and they couldn't see through it anymore. It looked like a screen, but it was in mid-air. Then came the words.

"Show us the hooded figure."

Within the flames, there was a shape that started to form. It took almost seconds, but the girls were bemused. Then, after a moment or so, the figure became clear. Smoke poured from the body and then mingled into the formation of the hooded figure. They recognised the demon from Proust's bedroom, and the three of them gasped. Then, the shape disappeared. The words came again

"Show us the beast."

Smoke billowed again and morphed into the clearest vision of the moon which they had ever seen. It was evident as they could see the dark craters, and the white of the moon hurt their eyes as their eyes pierced the vision with trepidation and dread.

A moment later, a flash of lightning and an almighty clap of thunder boomed over the house. The girls stood in horror as the vision now turned to the most horrific creature they had ever seen, standing over the body of their fiend, Ellie May. The beast's fangs ripped through her soft skin like a pair of sharp scissors, cutting a frail piece of cloth before throwing her lifeless body down with its massive claws. The beast let out a howl, and the vision disappeared.

The girls stood in horror at what they had just seen. Emsie fell to the floor as she fainted. This night had got too much for her, and her body had started to reject the night. The others stood there, looking toward their father for answers. None came—just silence. After a moment, their father floated back to his seat. He rubbed his head with his hands. He understood better than his daughters of what he had just seen on the vision. He paused. His hand fingers wiped the saliva from around his mouth, and he broke again. Then, he looked at the girls. Crystal was helping Emsie back to her feet and comforting her as Emsie had previously done for her at Proust's house. Then he spoke.

"Reingold has returned"

"He has found us."

"He will stop at nothing until he finds them."

The girls did not move. Instead, they looked at each other, mouths open. Who was Reingold? Who's us? Who are we? Finds what?

As the questions rolled around in their heads, their father opened a small drawer in his desk and pulled out a small box. It looked just like a jewelry box, but it was slightly bigger. They looked at it inquisitively as their father opened the book and pulled out a round, black object which turned gold before them. He held it up in front of him as if cradling the most important thing on Earth. He looked up at the girls before he mysteriously said.

"This is the first circle".

"I need to tell you everything. He is coming".

CHAPTER 7

THE UNDERSTAIRS

The girls were still bemused by the sheer fact that their father was a wizard. Was he a wizard? And if not, what was he? He made all those stuffed animals fly around his office and snarl and jump onto our laps. Also, if they didn't know what he was? Did anyone else know? The impact of this night was playing heavily on their minds. Their precious minds had stretched because of the bizarre happenings of the night. The very core of their capabilities was in question.

Their father was leading them down the wooden understairs, which was always locked. They were never allowed to play under the house as children. They never wished to. I mean, can you imagine all the spiders and small insects which lived in the dampness of the understairs?

"What's under the house?" Crystal asked as she quivered under the arm of her sister.

"Not long now, and you will see for yourself", her father smiled at her and then turned his face away. She didn't see that as his face contorted, so did his smile. She had clocked him. The fact that he seemed nervous about where they had made her more worried than ever. This fear was despite being in the presence of the man who she always relied upon to protect her. They were all worried. They were concerned about this night. What else did this night have in store for them?

"We are here", their father spoke in a low tone, like a whisper.

"Where?" said Leila

They stood before an old wooden door, which seemed to belong in the most horrific horror film of all time. The door looked like a hundred dead souls of men, heavily wrinkled and angry. They were the protectors of the understairs.

Their father knocked on the door with his bony knuckles, which sent a loud bang echoing into the void behind it.

"It won't be long now", he said, while the three girls waited anxiously.

Suddenly the door creaked slowly open. The girls peered into the darkness as a dusty mist flew through the cracks of the door. Their father held his hand flat, patting the floor, telling them to be silent and still.

"Don't make a sound!" he said as they all stood, waiting for what was about to happen.

"Don't move or make a sound", he said again.

Suddenly there was a flash of light like a lightning bolt which struck the door with the force of Mother Nature herself. The girls closed their eyes tightly, expecting a hundred horrors thrashing, which could crash through the door to attack them.

Through the mist appeared a slow and cautious shape. Finally, the sisters could make out a wisp which slowly mutated into the form of a person. It became a human man. His half-developed figure appeared before them, and his bony fingers massaged the wood on the door.

Behind the being, the chasm became more apparent. Their father turned to them.

"Don't worry. This is the protector of our world which stands behind this door.".

Crystal piped up.

"But Dad. What is behind this door? I can only see a tunnel."

Her father smiled kindly upon the three of them.

My children, you have to be equipped with the relevant means of defeating this evil. The ghost appeared over to their father and whispered in his ear. The girls couldn't honestly believe what was happening, but their father's presence assured them through their fear. Their father patted them down again.

"Don't worry. Everything is alright. I've been this way a thousand times".

He whispered back into the airy ear of the spectre, and they both smiled at each other. Then, suddenly, the ghost bowed down in front of the three girls.

"My dears", said the ghost.

"We have all been expecting you. I understand this is your very first time visiting us. I hope you will find what you seek"?

Their father turned around very sharply.

"If you want to gain access to this chasm, you must bow down before the protector of the circles and swear your allegiance".

The girls did as they were told and bowed down. The girls felt a strange but warming sensation cloud their minds. Then, in a peculiar unison, the three of them stood up. Their eyes had rolled into the back of their heads, displaying the whites of their eyes. They were entranced.

"We three so young and dutiful at this moment swear to uphold the order and secrets of the seven circles. We will protect the source of our beloved power until we cease one this earth."

With those words, they all awoke. Their father looked on as proud as punch as if they had done a recital in school. The spectre disappeared, vanishing. The wizard turned to the girls.

"The protector has accepted you into our realm, but we must pass quietly. I fear that Rheingold has become influential. Even though our domains are powerful, he may breach, like the thief that he is.

The girls felt the hairs on the back of their heads and arms prick up with fright and dread. The name Rheingold cast their short memories of their first encounter at Katrina Proust's party. Their father continued.

"Even though these corridors are for the powers of good, Rheingold is still a constant threat. Be on your guard. He has infiltrated the passageway between good and evil and between the underworld and this world. You must have your wits about you in your challenges. There is so much to tell you to prepare you, but I can't. You must go now and prove yourselves worthy. The master must equip you, and only he can provide the three of you with the relevant skills to defeat Rheingold".

Their father raised his hands and conjured a sphere of light.

"Promise me you will not fail?"

The sisters glared into the light, which headed straight for them. Leila noticed that her father was weeping. Before she had a chance to say anything, the sphere hit them and catapulted the three of them, hurtling down the corridor at a lightening's pace. In a flash, they had gone. The wizard stood there in the near darkness regretting that this night had finally come.

CHAPTER 8

NANCY PARTRIDGE

The night had taken a few twists and turns. Some of the townspeople went about their business, oblivious to the power of the Seven Circles. Others wouldn't have the mental capacity to understand. Some would never have thought it possible that a beast could be creeping around behind them, hiding in the shadows.

Here were some like Robert, the taxidermist, a protector of the Circles who possessed great and potent magic within the small sphere now tucked into his inside breast pocket.

Now being part of those secrets were his two daughters Leilah and Emsie. There was also his stepdaughter, Crystal.

However, some did not know the goings-on of this night. One of those was Nancy Partridge. She should have known. If she had known the life into which she had been married, then she would have understood guaranteed. She could have protected herself, and perhaps she would have survived the night.

If only such things were true. Suppose hindsight was a thing that you could willingly call upon to make those choices again.

If Nancy Partridge had known that the man that she had married was a wizard, then possibly, she could have protected herself from the beast.

If only!

Nancy Partridge had taken the opportunity, while her husband was busy finishing off one of his animals to go into school to finish on a few of her cases.

While the night was black, she sat at her desk in the school councilor's office. There behind the brown door, she sat, perusing some documentation, and signing the bottom before slipping the paperwork into the brown file.

The golden name sign on the open office door glistened in the lamplight. Dr N E Partridge, School Councilor.

As she sat in her office, she noticed that she was tired. She had also become suddenly quite warm. Finally, she had decided that she had done enough. Suddenly, the room lit up with the blues flashing of lights, and an enormous horn of fire trucks shot past outside of her window. She moved quickly to see where they were heading, but they had turned off up the street and had disappeared into the night.

Nancy knew that she was getting old, she was approaching her mid-fifties, but she still looked attractive.

Unfortunately, she had become drained recently. She slumped back into her chair, and she slid the brown file into her out tray. She stared into the darkness outside of the office and knew that she had done enough of a catch-up.

She sighed to herself quietly, and she opened the left-hand drawer and took out a white letter. She held it to her chest and paused momentarily. She looked lovingly at the picture of three girls who sat on her desk and started to leak a tear down one side of her face. She lay the letter down on the desk and recalled what she had read a few days before this day. She still could not process the fact that she was dying. She looked at the picture again, and her body filled itself with a warm glow of love.

Similarly, the girls had been through their torment this evening. She was unaware.

Nancy thought again that she had done enough work for today, and then on Monday, her students would present another set of challenges post-weekend.

She had always played such a proactive role in the lives of her students, but she had been particularly supportive in one of them. Danny Rostrum.

Danny was a charming and helpful young man, seventeen years of age, who had gone through some challenges in his life. She had also thought that things may not have turned out so badly for Danny if his father wasn't so heavy-handed with him and that his mother hadn't have died a few years ago. Danny had been struggling with that and had turned to become extremely aggressive and violent toward his peers.

As Nancy switched off the light to her office, closed the door and turned the key to secure all the secrets of her dear students locked up in the cabinet in her room, she turned and pierced slowly up the school's corridor. As her high heels hit the floor, they made a scraping noise which squealed through her ears. She noticed the strip lights at the top of the ceiling had started to flicker.

Nancy had the feeling that somebody was watching her. She looked around very quickly to see if there was anyone behind. Of course, there were not. She thought that this was silly. She laughed to herself quietly. She was not in some horror film where the stupid innocent girl walks up the corridor amidst the flickering lights. In the movie, she would now be seeing a masked fiend, wielding a metal axe now running at her in a horrible attempt to cut her up into little pieces.

But Nancy Partridge was not in a horror film. She did not know what had previously happened to her husband, the taxidermist and her three children. So, she turned her thoughts from the horror film to the more mundane things that happen day in day out in her village in her town. Would her husband, the great taxidermist had made his usual effort for dinner? Would she be tucking into some special?

However, unbeknown to her, she was in her bespoke horror. Something was watching her. Rheingold, the necromancer, had sent a Beast, and there was unseen darkness around her. She did not know that Rheingold had pierced the boundary between the underworld and the natural world.

She had no thoughts of Rheingold, the Master of deception, the thief in the night. She had no idea or knowledge of her husband and the part he had played in tonight. She also did not realise that her three daughters were on their way, catapulted into some chasm. To be proven.

No, she did not know, and she could not comprehend what was about to happen to her on the last night of her life. Her feet tipped over the linoleum floor, and she reached in her pocket to get out her mobile phone. She wished to phone her husband that she was on her way home. She did this every working day. As she turned a corner of the corridor, she noticed something, the thought of somebody watching her which had grown ever so much. She looked around, frightened, and knew that someone was there in the distance behind the lockers. Who was it? Who could be there at this time?

"Who is there?" she yelled. She hopefully wasn't going to hear an answer. She held her breath for a few seconds, and her beating heart pounded in her ears. Then, she had to take another breath, and her body hurt as she exhaled slowly before taking in another shallow breath.

No answer came, just a harsh scrape of the beast's claws on some metal object. She stooped and ran half bent as if that would make a difference. She clambered around the corner and waited on her knees whilst peering around the corner.

As she panted heavily, she could see the shape of the massive beast who cautiously turned the corner by her office where she had previously stood moments earlier. She knew she couldn't stay there. She got to her feet and turned quickly.

With a gold flash, a mighty force threw her to the floor. She looked up and could make out a hooded figure in a filthy dark robe. She did not know that it was Rheingold.

"Who are you?" She screamed out, but there came no reply. Instead, she could make out the thumping sound of the beast's huge feet coming for her. She became suddenly motionless and frozen in the cold glow of his golden beam.

"Who are you?" she demanded again. Rheingold had his left hand aloft, controlling the powerful beam, and with his right hand, she started to pull back the hood that concealed his face.

"You wish to know my name?" replied Rheingold, his voice sounded like a lion gargling with nails.

"My name is Rheingold".

As he pronounced the last syllable of his name, a thick and muscular carpet of fur slammed into Nancy with a brute force that was unforgiving. The impact was so horrendous and profound that it killed her instantly.

In the dying moments of her oxygen-deprived nerves, she could see Rheingold disappear, and the beast stood over her body a few feet away. It was then that she noticed that her head had been taken clean off her shoulders.

Her eyes were closed ten seconds later.

They closed for the last time.

Chapter 9

LOVE GRAVES

The Beast stood over Nancy Partridge's dead body and sniffed at the carcass before licking the blood from the floor. Rheingold had disappeared, leaving the vast monster to eat his share.

Flash!

A silver flash shot through the school corridor, blinding the Beast momentarily. He lifted his paw to shield his eyes from the silvery glare.

Robert had appeared through the silver flash and had teleported himself through the power of his circle. He looked at the lifeless body of his true love, who lay dead on the linoleum floor, but he had no time to mourn as he knew that the Beast would not be long before he pounced.

He was right. The Beast stood firm yards in front of Robert and let out a howl so loud; it shook the glass on the nearby trophy cabinet.

"You will not defeat me!" Cried Robert.

The lycanthrope fell on his forefeet and pounced towards the small man who stood firm. Before the Beast could strike, Robert quickly pulled the circle out of his pocket and held it aloft in front of him. The circle glistened like black marble and shot a hurricane of wind towards the Beast, pinning him fast onto the wall at the furthest point of the corridor.

The Beast knew that he was no match for the power of even just one circle, but he tried again.

He clambered to his hind legs and howled again to intimidate the old man. Robert saw that the vast shape was hurtling at speed towards him. Robert fired shards of lightning at the Beast, but they all missed. He repeatedly missed as the Beast jumped onto the wall, floor and ceiling. Finally, the Beast was close enough to Robert to strike, but he did not. The Beast came to a total standstill as Robert sensed a golden chill behind him.

Rheingold took hold of Robert; his bony skeletal hand blocked the circle, which sent it tinkling, lifeless up the corridor before rattling on the floor finally. Rheingold had enough of a grip on Robert to render him helpless. He waited. He smiled at Robert, which turned into a regretful glance.

"You old fool", Why did you come here? You are no match for me even with your beloved circle".

He held his right hand out, summoning the circle into his palm. He did this effortlessly, and he still had a hold on Robert's body, which shrugged and squirmed, trying to break free. Robert knew that he was no match for the necromancer.

Rheingold held his bony finger underneath Robert's chin for a moment before suddenly burrowing it deep into Robert's throat below his ear, severing all significant arteries, sending blood spatter up the nearby wall.

Robert heroically still tried to punch the fiend, but he could feel a drain of his energy like a battery that used up its last charge.

Rheingold waited until the glassiness of Robert's eyes darkened, and he threw his lifeless body on the floor. The Beast sniffed around Robert's body, but Rheingold stopped him.

"You will not feast on him. I owe my brother that much".

With a golden flash, they both disappeared, escaping the carnage they had created—leaving the bodies of the two people who were so much in love but whose love could not save them.

The only remaining hope against stopping the evil of Rheingold was now in the hands of three unremarkable sisters.

End of Part 1

Acknowledgements

My heartfelt thanks to the pupils, parents and staff of these schools

Tywyn Primary School

Sandfields Comprehensive School

Dwr y Felin Comprehensive School

Glyncoed Comprehensive School

Ebbw Fawr Learning Community

Abersychan Comprehensive School

Special thank you to my Mam – My eyes

"I love you more than all the tea in China"

About the Author

Visit carldavidmclean.com / Facebook (@CDMBooks) for more information on upcoming titles. CDMBooks is a brand-new book company dedicated to writing and promoting books that people enjoy.

Carl David Mclean is an educator, author, and musician. His first book, Time to Take Back Control was his labour of love and was a direct result of his own experiences. He is committed to writing content that helps people who have experienced traumatic experiences.

When he is not writing, he is a loving father and husband.

Also written by Carl David Mclean

Time to Take Back Control: A Guide to Improve Mental Health and Wellbeing for a Strong, Healthy and Successful Life

TIME **TO TAKE BACK**

Control

LEFT VS RIGHT

A Guide to improve Mental Health and Wellbeing for a Strong, Healthy and Successful life

CARL DAVID MCLEAN

Coming in 2022

The Seven Circles of Rheingold – Part 2

Printed in Great Britain
by Amazon

84732477R00034